To Isla,
May all your Christmas
wishes come true!

Love.................................

Isla is ⇒**excited**⇐
Christmastime is here!

She says, "I wish for lots and lots of fluffy snow this year!"

Isla writes to Santa.
The letter takes her ages.

"Perhaps I've wished for way too much…"
(There are over 50 pages!)

Dear Santa,

Isla decorates the tree
with twinkly lights that glow.

Christmas
decorations

Look at Isla up on stage.
She's in the Christmas play.

She wished to make
her family proud and
have the greatest day!

The kitchen's very busy.
Isla can smell baking.

"I wish that I could eat that bowl of cake mix Dad is making."

Isla wakes at 5 a.m.
"It's Christmas Day!
Yippee!"

She runs downstairs to find a pile of presents beneath the tree.

Isla

To Isla

This jumper's really itchy.
She tries to grin and bear it,
but Isla really wishes that
she didn't have to wear it!

Isla dresses warmly.
Her wish for snow came true!

She's off to build a snowman now.
Perhaps she can build two!

Isla's sledging down the hill. "I wish I could *speed* up!"

Her wish comes true,
her sledge is *fast*
when powered by a pup!

It's after Christmas dinner,
and everyone is snoring.
Isla says to her best friend,
"I wish it was less **BORING!**"

Later, Mum asks Isla,
"Did your **BIGGEST** wish come true?"
"Oh yes," she smiles,
"that wish was being…"

" ...here with **all** of you!"

Do you wish for fun with friends,
or a family trip that never ends?
Whatever it is that you hold dear,
keep your Christmas wishes here!

I wish...

Written by J. D. Green
Illustrated by Julia Seal

Copyright © Hometown World Ltd 2018
Hometown World Ltd
1 Queen Street
Bath
BA1 1HE

www.hometownworld.co.uk

Follow us @hometownworldbooks

ISBN 978-1-78553-965-7
All rights reserved
Printed in Italy
HTW_PO201806

put me
in the story®

Bestselling books starring your child!
www.putmeinthestory.co.uk

SANTA
STOP
HERE!